and then there are those who live in the back of old books
david macpherson

and then there those who live in the back of old books
Copyright 2020 David Macpherson
All rights reserved
macphersondavid607@gmail.com
100pagedash.wordpress.com
On facebook David's group is Dave Macpherson is a Writing Stuff.
Instagram DavidScottMacpherson

House of Hate by Dorothy Fletcher

Mikey was squatting in the open spaces of a gothic nurse novel. There were a few blank pages in the back, empty and inviting. The yellowed pages were clean enough and didn't have stains. He unpacked and now it was his, as much as any place ever was. He worked on his art in peace.

Terrence, who taught him how to live in the back of books, also explained how to eat punctuation. Mikey only ate the commas. These gothic romance things were always lousy with commas, the sentences were ripe with them. They pulled off the lines easy and tasted sweet and juicy, with the syrupy ink running down his chin. No one would miss the errant punctuation, of course that's considering that anyone will read this any time in the future.

He heard of some squatters eating whole paragraphs, or full appearances of secondary characters. These squatters considered it perfectly acceptable to eat as much from these lousy books as they wanted. They could not believe that these were the kind of books anyone would ever want to even notice, let alone read. But that was not Mikey's take. Why risk getting caught trespassing? Also, why ruin the book?

Most of the days were busy with his drawings of carrion birds. He sometimes saw them flying at the top of the book, circling the page numbers near the edge. When he was tired or distracted from perfecting his art, he noticed he was drawing portraits of woman he remembered from before. Women he had passed on the street. They had their hair well cropped and their makeup thick and precise. He crumpled those sketches and let them pile up on the bottom of the page he was using as his studio.

There was one day Mikey was foraging for commas in the seventh chapter and he returned to the back of the book later than usual. He saw movement so he hid behind an unclipped coupon for the purchase of further gothic novels.

He noticed a woman hunching down, smoothing out the drawings he had crumpled. She looked at each sketch before placing them gently into a pile. Mikey, from where he was hidden, could not see her face. But there was no way he could miss her nurse uniform and the blue cape.

It took some time but all the pictures he didn't care for were smoothed out. The woman, looking like a nurse, went through all of them one by one. She pulled out a few, making another small pile. She picked up the small pile and headed out into the body of the book.

Mikey never saw her face and he never did figure out which pictures she took. He discarded them as so much rot, so they were fair game for the taking.

A while later, Hire came over to the book with a proposition. Hire and a bunch of the punks squatting in an anthology of 18th Century Russian Poetry were starting a band. They needed some art for their flyers, if they ever got to the point of gigging out and thought Mikey could kill the posters. Mikey wasn't sure, he was pretty focused on his drawings of carrion birds and didn't know if that was going to be a good way to excite people for a band.

They talked for a bit, ate a few exotic pieces of punctuation, not as much for the taste but for a desire towards variety. Mikey mentioned the nurse he saw rummaging through his discarded art. Hire couldn't believe it. "Characters don't come alive. You read them, you imagine them as real while reading, you might even snuggle up at night against a warm paragraph perfectly describing them, but they don't come around looking at drawings."

Mikey agreed but didn't know who she was. It bothered him. "I looked around, and there is no sign of someone else squatting here. It's like she disappeared. It's nice that she isn't causing a scene. It's nice she found some of my work good enough to take along with her. But man, who is she?"

The days went on and Mikey realized he had to find somewhere else to be. He packed up his kit and went to the big old anthology where Hire was. There was plenty of room there.

His art changed. He was still drawing carrion birds, but now they were perched on the shoulders of faceless nurses, their capes blowing in the wind. He made many of these, started adding strong color and playing with composition. There was definitely improvement in his work.

The band never happened, so there was no need for performance flyers. Mikey did not crumple up and throw these new drawings out, which was a unique development. He kept them safe between a piece of folded cardboard. He carried them with him from squat to squat, as if he was keeping them for somebody, he was sure to see again.

The Last of the Mansions by Dorothy Daniels

Old moldy paperbacks, usually romance or historical genre novels, allowed many wild animals to roam in peace. No one was going to open up these fetid books, which allowed the wildebeests and the ocelots and other exotic animals to find a relaxing and pleasant habitat. The books were warm and safe and offered plenty of words and punctuation for the animals to graze on. And Hayden hunted them. Cured them, their skinned flanks hanging down from floral paragraphs. This was all just to practice for the big game, the one foe he truly sought.

Hayden, in another life, was a beer swilling, weekend hunter. His dad always took him out to get bucks or mountain goats, even if the license was out of date, even if the calendar whispered that it wasn't hunting season. He fished with an unauthorized net and ate the results. His father was a man who reeked of gunpowder and Lucky Strikes. His old man believed in getting whatever he was able to swipe with gun or seine net.

If Hayden's old man was privy to the knowledge that you could live in the back of books, that's where he would be. Living and causing havoc with the other squatters. Best for everyone that he never knew about this.

When Terence showed Hayden how to enter forgotten books, the first thing he wanted to know was how the game was. "There's animals, sure," Terence said, "but no one I know hunts them. Some have eaten the animals, but I wouldn't call them hunters, I would just call them hungry squatters."

"But I'm not just going to be sitting on my ass all day, eating overwritten prose and just staring at the yellowing paper, am I?"

"You're living, and you're out of the elements and can live off of the punctuation and words, so it's not doing nothing, Hayden."

Hayden didn't believe that. He wanted to know more about the animals. Terence sighed and told him,. "I don't know how they got in, but they are here. They don't bother us, because we don't bother them. Zebras and African animals like wildebeests and big cats and a few squatters told me about a really enormous deer. I think it's called an Irish Deer. Yeah, I think that's it."

"Wait a minute Terence. I've heard of Irish Deer. That's an instinct animal. They don't exist no more."

"Roaming in books must be good for the species because there are animals living in the collection that are on the extinction list. Irish Deer, a couple mastodon, and I think even a dire wolf was spotted. "

This excited Hayden; he struck into a large smile and could not speak. "A dire wolf. There is a dire wolf stalking about these old paperbacks? I'm sure he's a hazard, I'm sure I could bag him."

"Hold on now," Terence said, putting his hands up, "no one said it's a hazard. It minds its manners from what I hear. There has not been any encounter with the dire wolf and anyone who has found themselves living in these parts."

Hayden didn't hear that. He stalked off. He used a half parenthesis as a slingshot and gathered all the colons and periods he could wrest free to use as the ammunition. He practiced for a time in the back of an off-color joke book. He hunted other animals and got the feel of the weapons and terrain. He then set off.

He first got the trail in the third chapter of an Executioner novel. He followed the signs of the dire wolf through romance novels and well received collections of short stories until finally he had the thing cornered by the broken spine of a gothic romance novel. He didn't even bother to know what book he was in.

The dire wolf was drinking the ink from an expository paragraph. It was large with broad shoulders. Its snout was flattened out. The ears were smaller than he thought they should be. The fur was a glistening gray and there was script written on its sides. There was a good deal of writing on it but one passage was larger than the others and Hayden read it easily.

He spoke out loud, He supposed he was speaking to the animal, as if they were sharing a bedtime story. "Rivers and the inhabitants of the watery element are made for wise men to contemplate, and for fools to pass by without consideration." The dire wolf heard and turned its head toward him. Hayden took out the parenthesis slingshot and placed one part of a colon in the cradle.

The dire wolf bared its teeth. Hayden pulled back and aimed. Then it occurred to him that he knew that passage. His father said it to him as they went hunting. It was from the Compleat Angler by Walton. His father loved that book. He told Hayden that once. Hayden later learned it was easier to love books and passages than children.

With a lowered head, he returned his weapons into his sack. The dire wolf loped past, close enough to enrobe him in its odor of musk and newsprint.

Hayden built a house in that book. He never found reason to leave.

Horizontal Secretary by Amy Harris

The women in the band lived and practiced in the back of a sixties sex novel. It was easy real estate to get. Not many of the punks who opted to live in pages of forgotten, yellowing books chose the sex novels to squat. They were in lousy shape, made from rough coarse paper. And besides, they were lousy sex novels with ridiculously ludicrous covers.

Pags moved into Horizontal Secretary because she couldn't believe a more sexist unpleasant book existed, it had the cred of ultimate irony. She enjoyed living in the book, eating the naughty, slightly risque passages. They were filling, but did have an odd taste, but Pags was willing to believe that she invented the aftertaste as a form of feminist criticism.

She spent her days playing her bass. She was getting good enough to be bad and wanted a band to play out with. "Are there places to play out around here?" she asked Terence, who was the person who introduced most of the people to the style of book living.

"Sure, sure. When folks get together for a gathering, a birthday, someone celebrating getting a job in the bigger world, there are always a few of us who play some music. The anthologies have mostly weekly gatherings. We don't have bars or clubs, but there is always a gathering to hear music or sometimes people will read poetry, but mostly it's music. Which suits me."

Pags saw some of the bands, mostly punk, over the next few weeks. She decided that she wanted a band. But just women. A good old feminist punk band. Punk and women work well together, mostly because women look good in distressed leather jackets and off key chords.

She started looking for women to invite at the weekly gathering in the back of an anthology of american short stories. She didn't care if they could play, she just wanted women who looked right. They could learn to play, or hell, they could learn to not play. It was punk after all.

The first person she asked was a young yellow skinned girl named Karen. Karen didn't like the book she was just living in and knew a couple chords on guitar. She moved into Horizontal Secretary the next day. Karen invited her new girlfriend to share the space and she, Kayle, was volunteered to be the drummer.

"I get to bang things?" She asked and found a wicked smile on her face. She didn't have a kit, so she made one from what she could scrounge in the book. The lower-case ells became drum sticks. She used a kay as the drum base and placed dashes on them to use as drum itself. It didn't have a thick sound, it was thin, but for a do it yourself kit made from letters and punctuation, it was punk enough.

A woman who was foraging through the book was enticed to stay and be the lead singer. That was Tara and her raspy delivery was perfect for what they were attempting to achieve.

They practiced for weeks, for hours at a time. They were still awful, but they had accumulated a bunch of original songs that allowed them to be loud and to play fast.

After one three-hour rehearsal, Pags wiped the sweat from her brow and announced they were ready to play at one of the weekly gatherings. They were going to kick some chapters and leave all the rest speechless. "Now all we have to do is come up with a name."

There was a silence as all present considered the importance of this next step. The naming of a band is one of the premier decisions one can have. You are born, you went to school, you had a band with a great name, and eventually you died. This is the shape of the life that you can almost imagine having when you are told, "Now all we have to do is come up with a name."

Kayle broke the pause and said, "The Consequences." There was no comment after she said this, "I always wanted to be in a band called the Consequences."

With no other comment on her idea, that name died an indifferent death.

Pags said what she was thinking since she started the band, "Well we live in the Horizontal Secretary. We should be called that. Horizontal Secretary. It's a critique as well as being memorable."

Karen bit her finger and looked down. Tara said, "I don't know Pags. You're into it, I can tell. But I don't know."

"What. What don't you know?"

"Well I don't know if it's a good name. I mean it's where we live, right? It's our location? It's our address. Like we are the band 473 South Main Street. We ain't Secretaries. We certainly are not horizontal. I don't want people getting the wrong idea about us. Either being naughty or unoriginal."

Pags took a deep breath. "No. It's pretty fierce. We are thumbing our noses at the whole hypocritic society. We might live here, but that's part of the fierceness."

"Nobody's Miss. We can be that. Nobody's Miss," Karen said. There was no response. Only the angry hum from Pags and Tara glaring at each other.

Kayle swallowed and said, "Bra Burners? I know it's dated, but it's still kind of cool, I think."

This went on for an hour. Karen and Kayle gave up lame suggestions and Pags and Tara just glowered.

Finally Tara said, "I guess we can perform with no name."

"Yeah," Pags said, "That could be alright, I guess. I guess."

Tara moved out of the book two days later. Karen and Kayle left for a book of their own somewhere down the shelf soon after.

The next weekly gathering, Pags performed with her bass, singing along as best she could. Her set was made of covers of the Runaways, the Slits and Bikini Kill.

She plugged her bass in and said into the microphone, "Hey, we're the Horizontal Secretary." She looked around and briefly smiled before she put her scowl back on and started the first song.

Darling, It's Death by Richard S. Prather

Terence took Pickup on a tour of the books he could live in. Not really a tour, because tour makes you think that these are prissy well to do snobs who are only slumming when they decide to live in the back of books. Terence wasn't giving a tour. He showed Pick up a few places he could squat for a while or longer.

"You want to live in the back of these old beauties," Terence advised as they jumped from yellowing paperback to yellowing paperback.

Pickup didn't care where he lived, as long as the cops didn't find him. They hadn't started looking for people in books. He did hear that the cops cornered this dude named Philly, who was lying low in a gatefold of an old double album LP, so it wasn't unreasonable to consider that books weren't always going to be that perfect olly olly oxen free safe haven.

Cops are illiterate idiots. Books are the last place they'd look for Pickup.

Terence probably thought he was just another dumb punk looking for a place to write his zines, scribble his art, foment his useless political ideology. Dumb sons of bitches.

As if a quiet place to hole up should only be for the wanna be artists and the lost souls who forgot the adage about cleanliness. Damn. Pickup thought the books, with the mildew and the yellow disintegrating pages, stank, but they were nothing compared to those who nestled in them, in the back pages, living a forgotten life in a forgotten literature.

He gave Terence enough line to sound sincere. Terence kept on talking "For the first-time squatters, the newbies, I recommend bunking down in a big book with other people in it. There are tricks to learn, like how to eat the punctuation and how to jump from book to book. Others can train you better than I can on this quick walk through. Also, let's be fair, as much as we say we are loners, living in the back of a gothic romance novel or a locked room whodunnit can get very isolating. For that reason, I always invite new people to stay in a large anthology of poetry, we have many, where there is already a community. It can help with the transition from living in the usual world to a literary one. Well a bookish one, at least."

"You got any hardboiled detective novels. I can see myself living in a hardboiled detective novel."

"Yeah, we have a few. Not many. But I think one is vacant. Not a good book. In plot or in condition. Lot of water damage. Makes the punctuation taste funny." Terence took him to the book and Pickup made it clear he was ready to be left alone. Terence left.

The first few weeks in the book, Pickup lost weight and became twitchier than usual. He couldn't believe he was eating semi colons. They tasted nasty. But if he ate enough of them, and the commas and whatnot, he didn't have as much hunger. They weren't a steak. Hell, they weren't even a radish.

He was sure the cops were coming for him. He heard sirens whistling through the random pages.

By the second month, Pickup was used to eating and living in the book. He didn't bathe, which probably made him as stinky as the punks in the other books, but that was okay, because he never saw them.

Almost never saw them.

This one guy in a leather coat and long graying beard came every now and then. To see how Pickup was getting along. To try to make small talk. To compliment him on his choice of books. That kind of nonsense.

The guy's name was Russ. Though Pickup thought of him as rust. He was just as annoying and corrosive. All that fake kindness.

Rust came to visit one time too many and Pickup couldn't take the smile and the kind inquiries. It was just too much fakery. Pickup had a bunch of quotation marks he was saving for a later meal and just began tossing them at him.

Pickup was a good aim. That's what got him in this trouble in the first place, that his aim was too good. The quotation marks hit Rust over and over, some drawing blood. "Get the hell away from me. I ain't no joke, so scat."

"Damn. Damn. You got one crazy way of, damn." Rust said more, but Pickup didn't catch it because the bleeding man was finally leaving.

When he was completely gone from his book, Pickup sat down and sighed. Finally, he was allowed some peace. He closed his eyes and slept.

It was about two months further down the line when Russ came across Terence at one of the weekly gathering folks have in the big anthologies. "Hey, Terr, can I ask you about this punk Pickup, living in a detective book."

Terence nodded, "Yeah, Pickup. I heard he was tough on you, gave you some scratches. That's not right. Hope you're alright."

"Yeah, yeah, nothing serious. Left some blood stains on a copyright page, but nothing awful. The thing is, I checked on him again, and he's gone. No one knows where he is."

"Don't worry about it, Russ. The guy was a one of those nasty types. Sorry I offered him a space. But he's gone now. He hightailed it. There are some people who can never stay settled."

"I don't know, he didn't seem the type to be moving on. He seemed anchored. More than settled. He seemed set. Like cement."

Terence gave a smile and a shrug. "I don't know what to tell you. I don't think he'll be around to hurt you or anyone else. Like I told him back when I showed him how to live here: some folks aren't cut out for the literary life, or at least the bookish one."

The Bridge of Strange Music by Jane Blackmore

Maxwell didn't like being called Max. His name was Maxwell, it was something he was proud of, each syllable of his name meant something to him. But still people called him Max. Or Maxy. Or My Man Max. This was one of the reasons that he began to live in the back of paperback books. You can be social in a punk way and socialize with the other book squatters at the weekly get together in the 19th Century Literature anthology. Too many people talking to him and getting his name wrong.

He squatted in the back of a novelization of an episode of a forgotten sitcom from the 1970s. Who would visit someone living in a book like that? A lot of people it seemed. There were people crossing through to a better, more habitable book, or folk just checking in on Maxwell.

He could live on the punctuation and mind the quiet if he only was allowed to. Living in the backs of books should be off every map. But everyone makes new maps, its what people do.

Maxwell approached the Terence, the man who runs this whole thing, and said, "I just want to be left alone so I can say my own name to myself, I know what I'm called. I might have to go back to the world where no one cares about me enough to notice. I thought living in books would give me that anonymity."

"Maxwell," Terence said slowly, luxuriating on each of the syllables, "you are a person who wants a job."

"First I get all these people annoying me with talking and now you spit in my face by saying I should work in my life. I don't need this Terence."

"No Maxwell, no. That's not it. I will hire you to work for the common good. We need a guard. A security guard to watch a book. Just a gothic novel that no one bothers, but with this book, we like to keep it that way."

"You want me to hangout in a book that no one visits and make sure no one comes by? Send them on their way? That's it?"

Terence thought about his next response before he spoke. "That's it. Make sure no one comes into the book. No one goes near that book, we have it set up that way. No one comes into the book, no one comes out."

"Wait, are people trying to escape from the book."

"No Maxwell, "Terence laughed, "Nothing like that. Every now and then there is a book that doesn't do what it is supposed to do. The narrative changes. The font morphs. The characters materialize and cause havoc with the way the story should go. We have culled those bad apple paperbacks, but there are a few books that we just like to keep isolated. We don't want people there and that the oddities stay in that one book. But primarily, it is just you in the book by yourself. Stay in the last three pages, they are blank and safe. I rather you don't forage the book for punctuation to eat, so I will bring a basket of commas every couple days if that's okay."

Was it okay? It was all he ever wanted from the world. To be left alone and not have to worry about anything but the dream of solitude.

He was given his three-page beachhead and he began the solitary life, the isolation he desired.

The job didn't disappoint. No one called him Max. No one called him anything. No one ever showed up. What an amazing job, and how unprecedented to say amazing and job in the same sentence without detached irony.

The idea that they needed to guard this forgotten book in a large collection of forgotten books was unprecedented. But the object was to be alone, and here he was alone. Someone representing Terence came about and gave him the best, juiciest commas he ever ate. The guy dropped off the basket, asked if he wanted to talk, play cards, be social, and when Maxwell said no thanks, the guy smiled and left.

Once a month, someone stumbled by and Maxwell simply said, "Not a good place to be."

The unwanted person usually got the idea and left while issuing apologies. This was a fine life indeed.

He was mostly asleep when the heap of words shambled out of the middle of the book. It was a swirling mess of clauses and overheated passages. It bubbled out character development on its skin like abrasions or lesions. Whole chapters were captured in its guts. It had a mouth with sharp teeth of transition sentences. It's eyes were question marks twined together like old rope.

Maxwell was now awake as he witnessed it coming toward him. It was large and its end trained behind him like a formal wedding dress. It stopped in front of him, raised its body so that all the words and thoughts eclipsed above him.

It then slid to the side and headed past Maxwell, aiming to the way out of the book. It's leaving, Maxwell realized. "Hey. You. Stop right there!"

The morass of words stopped and slightly pivoted. "Yeah, I'm the guard here. And I keep people out, not bothering you, and you ain't going out to bother people. I am a crappy guard. I'm here just for the quiet and the namelessness of the place, but don't be trying to go. I'll rip you apart letter by letter. You won't like the way I edit you into a useless manuscript. I'll turn you into a passage that even Hemingway will think is underwritten."

The shambling mass of words undulated a sheen of adjectives and edged toward the exit.

"No," was all Maxwell said. "No. Go back. Now."

There was no movement. Then, without turning, the thing reversed and returned to the middle of the book. Maxwell watched the nearby pages for a few minutes and then closed his eyes and slept with a satisfactory smile.

A while later. Maxwell took a day off and visited the big anthology for the weekly gathering. There was music and attempts at dancing. Most folk left him alone. But those who talked to him called him Maxwell, to the man, without having to be told to do so. He was Maxwell. When he said farewell for the evening, he meant all that the words could imply.

He returned to his forgotten book and all the restless words that needed his presence.

The Myopic Mermaid by Carter Brown

Lucas and Flick were not lovers, but they acted like the old couple everyone assumed them to be. They came to the books together. They lived in the back of the same book very comfortably. They entertained visitors to the old yellowing thriller they squatted in with kindness and music.

Flick was the music guy, playing a beat-up Stratocaster. It was not a good guitar, but what punk wanted a good guitar? Living in books, sound echoed in strange ways. It bounced off paragraphs and reverbed on chapter headers. It was one old guitar, but it sounded like a DIY orchestra.

Not many people visited them in their book. Flick wouldn't say it, but that was because of Lucas. Lucas was the other kind of classic punk. The agitator. The disorganized community organizer. He spoke on length about what was wrong with the world and came up with plans on how to fix it and then he jumped right to the part where he complained at length about why his plans failed and why people let him and the movement down.

For a while, because the back of the book was several pages of blank, they had another squatter taking space with them. A guy named Mikey, an artist who was always drawing pictures of nurses. He said he ran into one in one of the books and can't stop drawing her. He was good, keeping his space clean and his voice low. He didn't last long.

Mikey approached Flick when he was by himself. "Man, I've got to split. That partner of yours has got to watch himself. The way he talks."

"What talk, ain't we the kind of people who talk the way we want?"

"Sure, yeah, course. But come one. We got a nice thing here. We live in books. We pay no rent. We eat punctuation. We meet once a week for the gathering, but for most of the time, we got the world to write or draw or play the guitar. Why mess with that? Why does he have to make a fuss about Terence and the others running this? There's no need. Organizing against the man is what we are about, but Terence ain't the man. He's just a guy. And all Lucas's talk is making me uncomfortable."

"Oh, come on, Mikey," Flick whispered, not noticing his lowered voice. He hardly brings that up."

Mikey tossed his pack on his shoulder, "That's your problem, Flick. You do not hear it because it's like living next to an elevated train, after a while you just don't hear it. Well, there is a lot of books, and I don't have to live by the train. See you around."

Lucas came back from foraging for edible punctuation a time later, and Flick heard it. Started hearing it all the time. "Yeah, eating punctuation. The commas ain't bad, but don't eat all from the same part of the book because you can't throw off the book. Why is that? Because Terence said that you can't. And why can't we eat the animals roaming these books. People say there are animals roving about and we don't eat that, but umlauts and question marks. Is a way to make us hungry and docile. Eat the bad punctuation and just listen to them. We need good sandwiches and maybe a couple apples to make us think smarter, that' what we should do Flick, we can...."

It was a long drone of complaint that Flick had never been aware of.

The droning playing at him and he thought of splitting too, but it was Lucas and they were always together. They jumped box cars long before they jumped paperbacks. How can you cease that type of history just because you suddenly realize that he talks an endless patter of nonsense? But the noise. The useless talk. How was he able to ignore it for so long?

Flick played his guitar more and louder. Lucas just thought he was focusing more on the music. He didn't know it was a buffer of sound.

It was the afternoon of some undetermined day when Mojar came by for a visit. Mojar was one of the people who walked next to Terence and spoke to him in private.

Mojar listened to Flick's guitar and ate their punctuation. She told some funny stories about punks living in books. One of them was about an all-woman punk band that never played out because they fought over what is an appropriate name. Everyone found it amusing. Mojar could tell a tale.

She folded her smile away, in storage for later perhaps, and said, "We can't have this type of talk. This undermining talk where you question us living here the way we do. You can speak what you want, but you are making people uncomfortable and we rather you just cool it a little. I'm sure you understand. It's a small community and we have to live peaceably together."

Lucas was silent. He should have been waiting for this, but his eyes belied a sense of ambush. He looked at Flick for aid.

"Mojar, that's not right. Lucas doesn't mean any harm. He's just questioning. Isn't that how we all turned up here in books, because we questioned a lot?" Flick asked.

"Questioning. Sure. But rabble rousing. Causing some to move to books further from you. It's a community, not just a group of individuals eating semicolons and playing their guitars. I don't want to change anyone; I just want them to be aware that words have consequences."

Flick looked at Lucas again, and he still looked shocked and mute. "We can go back and forth about the purpose of dissent all day Taja and we are not going to get anywhere," Flick said. "But the real question we have here is, what if Lucas doesn't shut his gob? Are you exiling us from the book we live in?"

Mojar paused as she thought on the question. "We don't want it to get like that. I wouldn't do that. We haven't because people are generally reasonable. We don't want to threaten or hold anything against you, just to remind you that you are not railing against a faceless tyranny, you are complaining about your own people."

At this Lucas leaned forward, his finger pointing, ready to have his say, and Flick put his hand up, ceasing him. "We understand," Flick said, "and we appreciate your opinions. Thanks Mojar. Thanks for coming and telling us how it is. We might see it differently, but it's nice to have you visit."

Mojar was a politician enough to know to leave.

As soon as she was gone, Flick stopped Lucas from saying anything by putting his hand on Lucas's cheek, "No. We ain't going nowhere. And we ain't changing. We ain't."

Lucas exhaled deeply and nodded his head. "Okay." And neither spoke again for the afternoon.

Look Back to Love by Vin Packer

Living in a book was the greatest thing for Tanya. When she was living in the world, she sold paperbacks on a blanket outside the park. Now she lived in a book. It was a Vin Packer, who was one of the Lesbian Pulp writers of the fifties and she could always put a post it on the book identifying it and getting a better price.

She started making book art when she realized that there were some books that never sold. Even at a quarter. She had to do something to help them move. She began to cut pieces out of the book or folding the pages that made entire chapters unavailable to the reader.

Broken books. That is what she called it when she placed them on the blanket the first time. With that name, they were still there at the end of the week, not a one sold. She made a colorful sign that read Book Art, and then they moved. How stupid people were. It was the same book, the same breaking, the same art. But sell it the right way and they will give five bucks for the privilege of owning a book that you couldn't read.

That level of dumb made Tanya flee to books, once she found out you can really live inside one. Terence told her about it and she was game. You live in the back of books in the blank pages and eat the punctuation. "Wait," she asked, "you eat the commas and periods and the ellipses and all that. So, your people aren't against altering the books?"

"Suppose not, but we don't hold up to destroying the thing that makes these all books. We like books, which is why we want to live in them in the first place," Terence said.

Tanya said, "of course of course." And already planned what she would do. She picked a nice comfortable book with plenty of space in the back for her bed roll and a few cans of paint. She didn't clear the paint with Terence or anyone else, but figured no one would ever find out, if they did, they weren't going to mind too much.

Mind too much? Best if she just did it and didn't get noticed. Which didn't seem right either. She was making art here, and why would you want to not have art noticed? Isn't that exactly the thing art rails against, the throngs and masses of those not noticing anything?

The first thing she did was read the book several times, which was not an easy task. Someone buying a paperback from the rack, all they have to do is find an unbroken chair in the bus station and crack it open and read page to page. But if you lived in the book, the act of reading was a strange, exhausting task.

To read the book, she had to trek to the beginning and jump from paragraph to paragraph like a rock climber. She had to hold on to low hanging letters, such as the letter g or p, though g was always preferred because it was easier to keep her hands on it.

She read it, she understood it. She appreciated some of what the writer was trying to do, but mostly it was a pulpy romance. It was perfect for her art.

And then she destroyed it. She began painting over whole swaths of exposition with a roller dripping with white paint. At first, Tanya thought she might leave a few words still readable on each page, making a found poem, or an alternative story. But the thing with painting the way she was doing it, it was too freeing. The power of editorial obliteration.

She painted over three chapters when she rested the roller in the inner crease of the book, surveyed all she wrought and said, "Alright, new plan. Still art. Just a new plan."

She sat for days, thinking of what that plan would be. At the end of that thinking spell, she stood up and laughed. "Okay, back to work." And that's what she did. She worked at it.

When it was done, there was paint of one kind or another, covering every word of the novel. It was a new terrain.

She made flyers and gave them out at the weekly anthology gatherings. It announced that she created a new art piece and that guided tours were available.

The amazing thing about art is that people come out of their own books to see it. People came, not a herd but enough to make the tours worth it. Because she destroyed all the punctuation, people brought her commas and semicolons for her to eat, to live on.

The tour showed all the painted over words. "This was how I painted over this chapter." She went into the reason. "With this chapter, I felt that red paint was the way to go, and that is also why the paint strokes are so ragged. It represents the ragged nature of the characters whose plot you can't read anymore."

She would recount the plot of the book. Went into characterization, and meanings. But after a while, the telling altered. Soon the story she told was different from what was originally on the page. "That's alright," she said, "books can take new stories on them. They want the glare of interpretation. They dare you to remember the book wrong. They live for change."

Folks liked the tour. They told other punks squatting in books to check out Tanya and her art. Terence's helper Mojar showed up for the tour. Tanya was nervous, but it went over fine. "That was cool," Mojar said when it was over. "I don't know what the art was, the book or you talking about it."

"Can't it be both or neither?"

Mojar smiled at this question. "Well done, I was surprised how much I liked it."

"Thanks, that means a lot. It inspired me, I have so many ideas of what to do with another book."

Mojar's smile stayed, but it altered. It was smaller, more judicious. "Ideas are great. Inspiration. It's wonderful. But I think one book is enough. Don't you?"

"Yeah," Tanya said. "Yeah. You're right. I'm just. I'm just happy you liked it."

That night, Tanya knew she had to make more art with the books. Soon, people would stop showing up and asking for the tour. More art needed to be made. Just what it was to be, that wasn't clear.

She would stay at this book and give tours and talk about the book she erased.

For now.

The Feathered Shaft by Jane Arbor

Zee always found it humorous. It was funny that for a group of people living in relative isolation in the backs of books, spending ninety percent or more of the day in solitude, there was a hell of a lot of gossip. It was a veritable knitting circle. One with leather jackets and mussed hair, but not so different from the original.

Zee had to laugh when the stories about Rory finding human bones in his book fluttered from ear to mouth and on to the next ear.

Zee lived in one of the big anthologies, and that made her more of a city person than those living by themselves in a romance novel or in a copy of a German science fiction space opera series. Those folks visited the big books once a week and got their socializing and their news. That's when the gossiping happened. Spreading like a bad case of athlete's foot.

The first thing she heard was that in the middle of his book, Rory came across skeleton bones. Looked human, looked clean. Didn't know what that was about. Soon enough the story turned into full skeletons left in every chapter. Charnel houses of bones and gristle were discovered. One of the stories described the bones tied to the sentences, hanging down like wind chimes.

Then came the parts of these infected speeches where they explained what it meant. Some were killed in a fit of jealousy and dumped in this book, not thinking anyone would eventually squat there. The wild, thought to be extinct, animals that folk see from time to time went ravenous and munched on a few unexpecting punks. Rory is crazy and killed people from the outside world and left the bodies here, away from police and literary critics.

The talk inevitably became more ominous. That this was the work of those who sort of run this community. That it is Terrence and Mojar trying to create their perfect to the side world by whatever harsh methods they considered necessary. Dangerous talk. Of course, that's what talk does, turns sour. Turns into anger and blame. That's how words are. Nasty untrustworthy things said the woman who lived in a large book of French Poetry.

She lived around words, inside of words, which is why Zee never felt she had to use much of them. Why add to the thick atmosphere of words if you don't have to? She was a woman of action, for the most part, and instead of listening to anymore, she took the trek to Rory's book, a really moldering number.

"You're Zee, right?" Rory asked. "Is there anything I can do for you?"

"You have bones. Show me them."

Rory suddenly riled up and his back stiffened. "This ain't a tourist destination. This is not the world's biggest ball of string. These are the remains of someone and should be respected."

"You have bones. Show me." She looked at him from below her brow. She was not an imposing woman, but she didn't take it from anyone and that was always understood somehow.

"Are you representing anyone? Are you the mouthpiece? I didn't do anything."

"You talked too much. You told people that you found bones. People told people. I'm getting tired talking. Show me."

Rory didn't even shrug. His shoulders sagged. "Come on then. Wait long enough and there's going to be a crowd and I'm going to have to tour guide and show the sights. Come on, already. They're in the fifth chapter and that's kind of a hike from here."

It was not a huge trek, compared to the walks she had in Russian novels or science fiction epics, but she understood what he meant. There was something about the paragraph construction of the book that made the walking arduous.

They walked for a bit and Rory stopped suddenly. "Wait. They were here. They're gone." All that they saw was the end of a chapter. There were no bones, of course. Rory looked worried. "I'm not a liar. There were bones there. Bones enough for a family, a really large animal. I don't know. There were bones. It was kind of in a circle. I'm not lying."

Zee went a few pages either way and then came back to where Rory stood, turning in circles, like he was looking for car keys or a guitar pick. "You can't stop looking," she told him. "The bones are gone. They got up and left."

Rory stared at her. She said, "They were probably tired of being talked about and looked for. Bones don't want talk, they want a place to stay and fade away. Bones are smart."

She went back to the anthology and noticed the talk about Rory's book and its bones began to fade and stopped. A few weeks on though, someone mentioned the bones to a group that Zee was in.

Zee said, "Yeah, I saw them. They were bones. We got a group of people trying to live here. Can't we talk about that?"

We Burn Like Candles by Bernice Kavinoky

Veganism is not something you just stop because you live in a back of a book and live off punctuation. Being a vegan is a point of view. It's an attitude. It's the right attitude as far as Yolanda was concerned. Just because she didn't have the opportunity to eat products that came from animals, didn't mean that she was not a vegan. It was about making the world better, of destroying as little of the precious ecosystem by her presence.

She spent a lot of time thinking about how I would practice veganism if I live in a book. Here the food is punctuation. Then it became clear to her. It was evident what the right and wrong way to consume in this world was.

All of this was explained to Tara, a woman she found looking for permission to forage in her book. Tara was one of the few punks who refused to pick a book and stay. This subgroup found it against the lifestyle to put down roots or covers. They were lazy, against the concept that one should grow leaves and fruit. These foragers appeared at the edge of books and asked permission to pick any surplus punctuation. They slept where they were invited or in unoccupied books. Full of musty pages and unrecalled plot developments.

"What kind of punctuation do you want now," Yolanda asked when approached by Tara.

"Whatever you don't need. Semicolons are tasty enough. Or commas from run on sentences. I don't mind, as long as you can spare then."

"No. I'm sorry. I can't let you do that. Really, I'm sorry. I'm a book vegan and anyone who comes into this book has to follow the tenants of book veganism."

"Alright. Sure. What are those tenants? I'm not trying to upset anybody. Just trying to forage for food."

"Oh I know Tara, but this is a vegan book. We don't believe any piece of a book should be harmed. The book should be read exactly as the author intended."

"Intended? How do we change the intention of the book."

"We book vegans believe that any word or punctuation alters the meaning of the work. We are hurting the author's creation."

Tara laughed and then quickly ceased. She saw that Yolanda was not making a joke. "How is a comma or a ellipse changing the need of the author?"

"Every word, every piece of punctuation was the purpose and intent of the author. They didn't casually put down a comma instead of a colon. Each drawn out sentence meant something. Who are we to destroy that?"

"But these are forgotten books. They are not read."

"That's not the point. The point is that these are creations. These are things of art. They deserve to be preserved so that the story is what the author imagined."

"Have you noticed what kind of book you are in? It's a pulp romance. Burn like candles? You might not believe it when you look at me, but there was a time when I loved a pulpy romance. They are great. But I can assure you, that no one, not even the writer, cared about what happened to it after it was written. They wrote with no rewrite, didn't care what happened when it was submitted and went on to the next book. This writer wouldn't know if there was a missing paragraph let alone a digested comma."

"It doesn't matter what they believed. They created art. That art shouldn't be altered or edited just because we might be hungry."

Yolanda looked above her at the corner of the page. "I eat what isn't necessary. Look up. There are no page numbers. They aren't necessary. I've eaten most of them. And the letter type is fat and full of flourishes. I scrap away from each letter. I make sure that they still can be read. I just make each letter thin and austere. It's enough for us to eat. And we are preserving the text the way it was meant to be."

"You keep saying we, and us. You talk in plurals Yolanda. Are there any other book vegans living here?"

"No, right now it is just me. But the we is the book vegans that will be. I am speaking for a movement. The movement is still a stationary boulder on the top of a hill, but you know soon it will be set free and moving downward. There will be more than me soon enough. Why shouldn't I speak that way?"

"Yolanda." Tara spoke the name as a admonition. "Yolanda. You don't look good. You got hollowed eyes. You are thin like a fashion model trying for that heroin chic. I'm worried. You got to eat."

"I get enough. Shaving the letters, eating the page numbers, my beliefs. That's enough."

"You don't look like enough," Tara said. "I came for food, for punctuation. But I think you need what I have." She opened up her bag and took out a few parenthesis. "These are pretty good, I found them in a comic crime caper book, please take them."

"Taking that out of text changes the story. Changes the book. I can't take it, though thanks. I do have enough. Our beliefs. They are enough."

Tara left, but kept asking others about Yolanda and book veganism. No one had seen her for a few times and most people on hearing about book veganism indulgently nodded at her crazy belief.

Yolanda was not disturbed for several weeks. She moved through her book slowly, carefully.

Tara returned. She stood before the emaciated woman and opened up her bag. Tipping it, out rolled half a dozen ripe fat apples. "Eat. Please. Eat."

Yolanda took one in her hand. "A lot of these are processed with insecticides and other chemicals."

"Not these, Yolanda. I found them in their natural setting. I was foraging in a group of old school romance novels. No bodices. No gothic mansions. No nurses. Just people falling in love. None of our people ever claimed these books. Too simple, I guess. I was filling my bag with ripe commas when I bumped into a tree. There was a tree growing from the bottom of the page. It hid almost all of the text. Apple tree, course. I never heard of trees growing in books, but that just means I haven't explored enough books. There are a lot of apples. They don't hurt the book. They are just delicious."

Yolanda gazed deeply into the apple, "But you said the tree obscures the text."

"Just eat the damn thing already."

She gently bit into the fruit and the sweetness and unadulterated flavor made her cry'

Surfing Nurse by Diana Douglas

Pete had bags under his eyes. He yawned through every sentence he uttered. He couldn't stand the honking of horns, the playing of lousy pop records, the shouting of roommates, the hum of streetlights. Everything kept him up, he was tired.

He came to live in the back of books because Terence assured him that there were whole long stretches of books and genres that no one inhabited. "Nurse books. That's what you want"

"What are nurse books? Are they manuals?"

"No, nothing that helpful. Nurse books are romance novels. Young nurses go to a new assignment, sometimes in haunted houses, and they fall in love with the dark, deep young man. It takes about a hundred and fifty pages for them to realize that the passion they feel is not the Florence Nightingale effect and truly love each other. An evil aunt or governess tends to fall to her doom from a high turret near the end too, but not always. But the books with the evil aunt or governess tend to be more desirous as a place to live. I don't know why. It's like having a pool in a backyard, its just a real estate winner."

"I don't want anything that will have noise. I want to sleep."

"Alright," Terence said, "I hear you. Living the rural life in feral books is a better way to get quiet. But I have to say, sometimes the noise that keeps a person awake isn't coming from the outside, you know?"

Pete knew but didn't want to talk to this guy about his fears and regrets. He didn't want any of this, only a place to sleep. Sleep all day. Sleep all night. Sleep when he wanted to. Sleep so no one could tell him what the right way was to be. Sleep to stop the parents from complaining. Sleep to unlisten the punks explaining why this person is punk and this person isn't. Sleep of reason.

He found a nurse novel without gothic trimmings. Just a bland romance, one that took place on the beach. He was worried that the sound of the waves would keep him up, but Pete discovered that the sounds from the story are not the sounds of actually living in a book.

He heard other squatters in nearby books. People shouting hello at him and others. The trudging of stray forgotten animals walking through chapters, foraging as they went. He heard the crinkle of the pages in the wind. There was the slow insistent burn of the pages turning yellow.

It wasn't like traffic in the city. It wasn't a crowded squat with eight punks jostling against each other. It was a forgotten and unloved nurse novel. And Pete stayed up all the nights, and was awake all the days. He was more tired than ever.

He walked around the pages of the book. He took great treks through the chapters, pausing only to eat absently at a piece of punctuation. He never finished them, not even the tiniest of quotations marks. His appetite was kept up with his restful nights.

He leaned into short passages, pressing his ear against the bulk of the words and listened. He mostly heard nothing. Every now and then, during a racy part of the book, usually, he was allowed to hear a small hissing, like a tire letting air out through a small tear. But that wasn't a bad noise. It was like white noise. The kind of thing they would package in a gadget and give the insomniac a choice of calm sounds to sleep by: a gentle rain, small waves crashing, breeze through Spring poplars.

He found a page that was full of words. For a book like this, it was surprising to see such a long paragraph. It was the bulk of the page. There had to be a lot the author wanted to say. There must be a tremendous amount of deep-felt emotion expressed there. He leaned against one line, not thinking of anything, and all the words pushed back.

The words of the line squashed into the next word and into the next until there was almost no space between the words and the letters. It became a thick black splotch. There was no way to read it anymore, though to Pete, they still had a sense of being words. It couldn't hide completely that it used to be a sentence, a line in a lousy novel.

The next line, the one underneath the squashed one, was the next one. And then the one under that. He did all the lines of prose on the page until it was a jumble of black. It wasn't a complete wall, it still had a "letterness" quality. It took up only a small part of the page. Pete never realized how little the letters and words and sentences were of ink. It was mostly blank spaces. He supposed that what he read was not the words but the emptiness around them.

He sat down hard, gasping for breath. Pushing letters into black mush was harder work than he thought it should be. He looked at what he made. "I need to do more. This page needs more of this wall." When he spoke out loud, the sound echoed from all the blank page he had created.

He went to the next page and wrestled words into his arms. He then carefully walked to the mostly blank page and dropped what he brought. He picked up each word and pushed it into the black wall of ink. The next word and then the next. Crushed into the wall, becoming part of it. He then went back to the other page and burdened his arms with more words. Sometimes, he cradled up to seven words, but most times he was only able to fit four or five. When the words were larger, like "incontrovertible" or "psychotropic," he only was able to lug the one word.

He emptied out that second page. He went to the third. To the fourth page. To the ninth page. To the twentieth page that he emptied of words. All deposited at that one with the ever growing mass. He was making the wall bigger. But it was not completely solid. There was a large oval space in the middle of the page that he decided to not fill up with squashed words. "It's like a room," he realized. So he made a room around all that almost solid black. If that's what Pete was making, then that was what he was making. He didn't have to understand his actions, he just had to bring the words from the other parts of the book and shove them into the mass of ink.

It wasn't a surprise that not only a bubble of space in the middle of the page, in the lower left corner, a tunnel of blank page was formed. "That's how I'm going to get in there." He didn't realize the purpose of the tunnel or the large bubble until he said it out loud. "Oh." He said, wiping his brow. "Oh, I'm going to sleep in there. That's it, isn't it." He knew there wasn't anyone to hear this. But when you discover what the purpose of your labor is, you should say it out loud. You should let people know, that, "I've made the perfect chamber for quiet sleep." But wouldn't telling others be almost the opposite of what he was attempting.

When Pete collapsed at the edge of the page and looked at his work, there was hardly a word left in the book. There was a passage describing a sleek surfboard that Pete left unmolested.

The page he created was like a word balloon to a comic strip. In the middle of black was a bubble with a tail that he climbed through. He ate pieces of the black, it was rich with filling nutrients. He lowered his head and he could feel a vibration. As if the words were trying to find the right time to expand to its original shape. Pete understood that any time the words would explode. Verbs and nouns flying everywhere.

But the bubble was so quiet. It was the silence he wanted. He closed his eyes. And slept. He didn't dream about any type of words flying all over the empty book. He only dreamed of silence.

Halo for Satan by John Evans

Living in books is a lonely life, if you want it to be. In the backs of books, people are ready to be hospitable. To offer a place to sit. An ear to listen. A thought to share. And if they were lucky, a jug of wine to pass around. That was the case when Flick left his book and visited the big anthology of 19th century poetry, which was treated like a youth hostel. Everyone had a place to bunk up there. It wasn't homey, but the book was huge and had plenty of room. People tended to start their lives in books in that book, and then branched out to a paperback of their own.

Flick lived with his bud, Lucas. But Lucas was working on a project, some manifesto, and had people over that Flick couldn't stand. He knew Hire from the weekly get togethers. He was hoping that Hire had some time to talk, and to share that wine he always seemed to have.

Flick was in luck. There was a large bottle of cheap wine. They drank it respectfully, which is a nice way that both thought of chugging for it was worth, but thought it wasn't the right way for a good person to drink, even if it felt like the right way to do it. They talked about people they knew. Then they talked about drinking. That's how these conversations went.

"I heard about a punk, one of the earlier punks in books, who got drunk from words that went bad and fermented." Flick took an extra swallow after he spoke, and only then, passed the bottle to Hire.

"Yeah, I heard that too. Was it from that guy William?"

"I don't remember what guy said it, only that it was said. Punks with sunken eyes and five o'clock shadows, they all start looking like each other."

"True, true. Hell, we even look exactly alike. Which is weird. Here, your turn with the bottle. Don't want to be impolite. Now the story I heard about William was that he smoked up some of the words and they got him a nice high."

"Like grass? He was smoking dope."

"Yeah, that's what I heard. There were certain words, or maybe it was a certain kind of type combined with a certain tense, if you packed those words in a bowl, you got well and truly toasted."

"Maybe it was WIlliam, but I am sure I heard it was a certain patch of words, a paragraph, or a chapter that went bad and if he squeezed them, he got a nice kind of liquor. That's what I heard. He made jars of booze from squeezing words."

Mojar, the second in command to Terrence, spoke up. Neither Hire or Flick knew she was close by. "Well I heard it was fermented words, but he didn't squeeze it. He put it in a still that he made. He forced the fermentation. And I am pretty sure the guy was Al, not William. Al, who lives in Halo for Satan. He was the booze man, from the way it was told to me."

She held out her hand, letting them know that she would like a turn on the jug of wine. Flick had it and looked at the jug and then the waiting hand. He didn't like Mojar, or Terrence. They gave him and Lucas a hard time a while back. Nothing became of it, but it made it hard to give her the bottle. But he did. You didn't let a hand wait for something as communal as wine. "Thanks," She said.

"No problem."

Hire spoke up, "Al from the Halo for Satan book? That's impossible. A guy living in that book doesn't distill words into booze."

Halo for Satan was known as one of the biggest books for Holy Rolling teetotaling preaching. They had twelve step meetings all the time and folks who went to the books to dry out, to hide out from wants and desires would tumble themselves to Halo for Satan. Every community needed that kind of last stop. People came and went out of the book, but Al was the mainstay. The main man.

Flick agreed with Hire, "He's the king of sobriety. Hard to talk to when he comes around here. Everything is a chance to talk about his one day at a time and steps and how we are just not good enough to understand."

"People change, fellas," Mojar said, finally surrendering the jug. "That's what we pride ourselves on here in the books. The chance to change. I don't know for certain about how he got the booze, but he got it. There was one time, he was rampaging through every paperback near him. He was wasted. Wearing only a dirty pair of black jeans and a horned helmet. The kind you see in pictures of vikings. He was waking people up. Plowing through paragraphs. He had a string of words stuck to his feet. Those words smeared across the pages as he walked. That's how we found him. We followed his footprints. Never saw such a disrespect for words, and we all eat them. But a drunk in a book is a bad thing."

"So says the woman sharing a bottle with two punks in a book," Flick said. He tried to pull back his dislike for Mojar in what he said, but he wasn't sure if it worked.

She smiled one of those unlaughing smiles. "Yeah. But I wasn't tearing through books, ruining sleep and texts. Or at least, you don't know I have. A lady needs her secrets. Anyway. I talked to him. Actually, I dragged him to Halo for Satan, which was already a dry book. A woman named Mary ran it. She got him straight and he took to it. Became very adamant. A hard shell sobriety. Mary wasn't militant, straight edge enough. She went to another book to live alone. Al is like that. I asked him about how he made words into booze."

Hire said, "He didn't tell you. Course he didn't tell you. Why would he tell you about his old life."

"He did tell me. Funny. I was sure he wouldn't. But he told me. He said it wasn't the words. It was never the words. Can't get drunk on words, he said."

"Wait, then what did he ferment?" Hire said, pulling hard on the jug.

"No, I don't know," Mojar said. "He wouldn't say. He said I could figure it out, but wish I wouldn't. I tried, fellas. I don't know what in the books can do that. Can get you drunk."

Flick grabbed the wine and held it up, "Except for this. This works fine."

"Fine enough," Mojar agreed.

"No," Logan said definitively. "The guy I was thinking of was William. Yeah, totally. It was William. I don't know who you're talking about."

The Vampire of Moura by Virginia Coffman

Lora broke her leg falling off a top paragraph in the middle of the book she squatted in. She didn't like the book. Now she really didn't like anything about all of it. She landed badly, her right leg straight under her. She heard the snap long before she felt any of the pain. She realized what happened and swore.

She attempted a poor excuse of standing and collapsed once more. "Damn it."

She lived by herself here. She was happy about that. Well, she wasn't happy about that now. Now she wished that rat Walt was still with her. Actually, no. She never wanted to be with anyone like Walt again. She was through wanting and needing anyone else.

A shot of electricity ran through her leg and Lora gasped. Okay, maybe this once, she wouldn't be strong and want a man to rescue her. But that was the pain talking. And at that moment, the pain was talking quite eloquently and sweetly. Let it be the orator, when she was back and healthy, she could go back to smart thinking once more.

She crawled to the next page, pulling her body with her hands gripping tightly onto the paper. When she made it the bottom of the next page, sweat was blinding her. She greeted this new page with heavy, labored breaths. There was no way she was going to make it much further that way. And if she did, if she did make it to the back of the book, where her bedroll and her stuff was, what then?

She lived by herself. Alone in the isolation made by finally letting Walt go. Letting all the mean men go. Now she was panting and sweating in the middle of a book no one visited.

"Yeah, you can live on your own, Lora. You can make it yourself. You didn't know about living in books. You didn't know how to eat the punctuation. You didn't know much. And now you want me out. Fine. Good luck with all that." And that's how Walt left.

Damned if she was going to let his words turn out to be true. Damned if that was going to happen. She reached up and grasped some words above her. She ate on a letter W. She figured she should for strength.

She sat there unmoving for most of the day. Books don't get dark at evening. There is no change in the light. But anyone living in one knows when night shows up. She knew it was evening and that the pain was awful. "How am I going to get out of this," she said aloud. "How am I going to build a fire now?"

Those words woke her from the deepest part of the fog. Why did she say that? What could that possibly mean? She didn't want to make a fire? Did she? No, if she lit a fire, she would get folks' attention, but not before she was crisp and dead. The pain shot up her and she stopped thinking for a few moments.

Lora took a deep breath and said, "To Build a Fire." She smiled. That's a story. She read it in Junior High School. They made her read this macho nonsense. Of course they did. Guy in Alaska or some cold ass place. Just this guy and a dog. He does some stupid things and gets wet and begins to freeze to death. The whole story was him trying to start a fire and failing. And dying. The dog went off without him. "The hell with that. I want an animal that can carry me on its back." She laughed.

She was in that story. Without the animal companion. She was stuck in a story she didn't want to remember. She didn't remember it really well, but there she was. Her leg was broken and she was stuck in her mind in a dumb macho story.

"I'm in to build a fire," Lora said. "I'm in to build a fire. I'm in to build a fire." She repeated it on a tape loop of pain and exhaustion.

She closed her eyes and said, "I'm in to build a fire." She opened her eyes. And she was still lying on the bottom of a page, but it wasn't the same page. It was larger, whiter. The paper felt thinner as well. This was nice paper stock, not coarse pulp.

She looked over her and the text was tight and small. There were a lot of words on this page. You could eat on this one page for weeks. She was on the last page of a story or an end of a chapter. There was plenty of space between her and the bulk of text. She craned her neck and read the last line, "Then it turned and trotted up the trail in the direction of a camp he knew, where were the other food providers and fire-providers."

Lora laughed with recognition. That was the last line of "To Build a Fire." She was in an anthology with that story. "Stories are more true than you and me," she said, though not certain why and what that meant.

This was one of the big anthologies. Lots of folk lived in them. She shouted help and soon heard people approaching.

"I want to go home," she said before anyone arrived. "I want to go back to my book. And I want a dog. One that won't leave me."

A tall punk came to the page and she closed her eyes. They will fix her up, but she did it herself. She built her own damned fire.

Fog Island by Marilyn Ross

Tor, Bill and Dylan were zinesters. They knew each other from the other world. The world of streets and debt collectors. They discovered each other through the zine scene. Their work was similar. They wrote about living in squats and straight edge bands. All of them hand wrote their zines. It wasn't because a lot of the other zinesters hand wrote their zines, it was just it seemed like the way to go. Once, someone called Bill derivative in his zine design. Bill found the critic, broke into his place and set a sofa on fire. Served the idiot, what punk critic would have a fluffy sofa? Even if he found it by a dumpster. Punks sit in chairs or on boxes or on the floor, because who can worry about furniture when you have the latest issue of your zine to finish?

And that's why Bill had to find a different place to live, which was how he found himself living in books.

He thought it served his need for focus and he told Tor and Dylan about the world of words and punctuation. They both came. They were told that zines practically write themselves in this environment. Words not only dripped from the trees, hell, words were the trees.

Dylan took to it. He wrote about living in the book. In visiting other books. He was flying with three new issues, and enough stories and articles for any other zinester who might want another piece to fill it out the page count of their issue. It was like it always was.

Tor had a tougher time. "I like to write about bands and books. Actually, that was the name of my first zine, I did it when I was fourteen and discovered Jello Biafra and Celine. I needed to write about those things. Now, here we are in the land of books and I don't know."

"There are bands," Dylan pointed out.

"Sure, yeah, there are bands. But its all crap. Thrown together combos with borrowed equipment. If you thought the New York scene was filled with lousy bands, you've never lived here."

"Those folks are just having fun at the get togethers."

"That's not what bands are supposed to be doing. Bands are slaps in the face. This is more like karaoke night at the TGIFridays. And then there are books."

"What about books, we are living in them, that shouldn't be a problem."

"That's the problem Dylan. People aren't reading books. They're living in them. Books are houses and supermarkets. If I wrote about books here, it wouldn't be about the desperate need to read, to know, to understand. It would be more about writing about housing issues."

"Writing about houses and squats is a noble topic."

"So is living vegan and being self sufficient, but I ain't wanting to write about that. I want to write about bands, and there are only so many ways I can hand write the words suck and disappointing. And it kills me. One of the things I always loved was seeing a punk on a corner curled up with a well thumbed paperback. Now they are in the book and they ain't reading. This is the death of reading, living in books. It's like washing dishes at a Chinese restaurant. After the first week, you don't want to ever see a dumpling again."

Dylan rubbed his head, looked at his own papers, wanting to get back to his own thing. He was writing about this dude who went hunting for game in the books, crazy people doing crazy things, you want to kiss people on the lips for giving him such easy lay-ups. He never met the guy, the story was all third and fourth hand, but that was okay. Dylan didn't worry about facts, just the good story, and he was dying to get it down, and see how the letters and phrases turned out. He never knew. He felt like he was rolling craps every time he wrote. "Can't write about books or bands. Write about that. Write about what you are missing. What is wrong. That's righteous too."

"Nah, man," Tor said. "Nah. That's not my thing. I want to write in a positive or honest way. Positively honest." He left Dylan to his work, can't be bothered by a guy who was making zines. It was only polite, cause nothing pissed Tor off more than when another was pestering him when he was at his pen. He started writing about his childhood, high school stories. And he started another zine about his dreams. His dreams were chockablock now, strange and correct. He wasn't just writing the dreams, he was interpreting, too. The zine was Both Sides of the Goddam Veil.

Tor and Dylan should have been happy, but Pete was impossible to live with. He stank. He left his crap everywhere. He never foraged himself, just took the food of the other two who had. He had some crazy sense of privilege. He picked up girls just coming to live in books and hooked up with them right there in the book all three shared. He didn't talk to them. He never asked. He just did it.

They didn't talk to Pete about it. They tried but Pete had an ability to gloss over and not hear a damned thing. Dylan wrote about it in his zine. Tor had a dream where he was eleven years old and just started a new school and there was toilet paper stuck to his shoe for the whole day and no matter what he tried, he couldn't get it off. It was there as he walked home and kids pointing and chittering about it.

The thing that was the most galling: Pete wasn't writing zines. He was just underfoot. If he was doing something, making something, maybe it would be tolerable.

"What the hell, I got to move," Dylan said as a way of greeting.

"Way ahead of you," Tor responded. "I've been moved out for almost a week now. I came back now to pick up the last of my stuff. I want to leave no footprints."

"Man, I just thought you holed up in the middle of the book working on dreaming and recording. A man writing is something you don't pay attention to. I didn't think you split."

"Why think about it, just go. Split. If I can't write the way I want, I'm leaving the books, I might try living in Chicago, I've always dug the vibe there."

"I'm not done with books, just done with this one. But I understand wanting to leave books. I mean I might be able to write my zines, but no one reads them. They're just piled unloved in my bag."

And like that, they were gone.

It was a few weeks before Pete realized that the absence was permanent. He made sure to run into Dylan at one of the weekly gatherings a few weeks on. "Good riddance to you. Didn't even tell me you were moving on. I got you here, you know."

Dylan was having none of it. He was creating zines filled with unique words and punctuation. They weren't put together into any kind of narrative order. It was just a sampler of weird figures of ink. When the reader was done looking at it, or admiring it, they could eat the words and markings. It was a big hit. He called this zine "Eat Your Words." He was sharing space with a cute young punk who made killer sculptures out of page numbers. Dylan slept well in his new book and was happy, so he wasn't going to put up with Pete one bit.

"You told me about this place. But I came myself. I lived where I was and then moved when I decided that was the right thing. I am a grown man who writes zines and lives in books. I owe you nothing other than a nod of the head when I pass you walking by." With that, Dylan turned so that Pete wouldn't get any chance to reply and went looking for his girlfriend.

Pete was annoyed. Dylan didn't even give him the chance to roll in and yell and fight. That was the least Dylan could have done. Pete brought him in here after all, he should have stayed and been yelled at.

He went back to his book. He looked at the empty sheet of paper that waited for him. Pete had a lot to say. The next zine will be how friends are not friends. How people are ungrateful. He picked up his pen and brought it down close to the paper. He held it there for a few minutes. Long enough for his hand to get tired and the pen to quiver. He dropped the pen and tossed the paper into the air. It landed amidst all the other discarded things and detritus.

Wiretap by Charles Einstein

There are no stars or moons or heavens in books. There are the words: star, moon, heaven. But that's all they are, words. They have as much to do with the actual celestial objects as Air Supply or Barry Manilow has to do with actual music. You could spend a whole evening sitting in a sexy romp of a novel about cute dames and eavesdropping and you can gaze at the word moon. But that doesn't mean your eyes are engulfed by the moon. There is no waxing or waning. This moon never changes, never glows. There is no mystery in the letters. They are just letters. Things that we force with sheer will to have meaning. The moon, the real moon, doesn't have to try that hard. The moon is meaning, and far away.

That's what Phaedra thought as she looked at the word moon in the book she was living in. Her girlfriend brought her here. They were as in love as always. "But I miss kissing you under the stars," she said to her.

Des, her girlfriend, laughed. "That's romantic, but I'm sorry for being precise, but when did we ever kiss under the stars? We were in a taxi when we kissed for the first time."

"But there were stars out, above that taxi."

"No. By the time we were in the cab and heading back from the show, it was down. There were no stars. The sky was lemon. No stars. Just like here."

Phaedra shook her head violently, "There is a difference. A real difference. Somewhere in the night there were stars, and the moon and shooting stars and UFOs, but the good kind. That's what's missing here. I've been staring at this word that means the moon and it's nothing that makes me romantic or crazy or lonely. How can we live here without the moon?"

"I don't know Phae, I don't know. But I thought I was your moon. You are my stars and my gravity."

"That's so corny," she said, but her smile was like the shine of one of those suns she was just compared to. She threw her arms around Des and pulled her to her lips.

They kissed for a very long time. It was all they focused on, so they weren't aware of Tara tiptoeing past them and out of the book, on to other titles.

Tara didn't mean to eavesdrop. She was only doing her thing: scavenging for unique pieces of punctuation. She always asked permission to go through the book. She knew this book was inhabited but couldn't find the squatters. She went through most of the book before she heard Phaedra and Des. Tara was about to go to the next page, but stopped. She began to listen to the two women. She was fascinated about Phaedra's desire for celestial objects.

Tara never even considered the absence of stars. It never occurred to her to miss something that didn't mean anything to her. She liked seeing the light in people's eyes as they recounted a favorite story. That heavenly twinkle, but actual stars? They never burned for her. So when she first heard the two women speaking about stars and moons and such things that hung above most people like stage dressing, she was about to come out and say that it wasn't true. That there were such things in books. Not the words. Not a strangled metaphor for the things, but the things themselves.

The stars, she found in a sixties sex novel. The words of one whole chapter broke down into shining dots. Throughout those pages, Tara walked carefully through the hung stars of former diction. She couldn't figure out if they were a byproduct of decomposing words. When words finally die and molder, these tiny stars are what they become. Or could it be that this was not decomposition but a form of evolution, that this is what words turn into when blessed with time and chance.

Tara's hand brushed against one of these stars and it burned with absolute cold. She still carried the scar on the back of her hand. When she finally navigated herself through chapter and returned to words, she had to rest. Her face was burned red and it took several hours for her eyes to settle and allow her to see things that actually were there.

She was in a horror novel, as much as a story about drunken grave diggers against townsfolk is horrific, when she spied the moon in the back cover. People dressed in tailored pants and print dresses kneeled before it. She didn't get too close, but was surprised by how these older people were all dressed like they were from the 1940s, or were survivors of a swing music revival band. They just kneeled in front of this mostly full moon. Occasionally, one of them would genuflect, with forehead touching the ground. It could have been a play of the eye, but Tara thought that the moon glowed a little brighter when one of them bowed down.

She spent the next few weeks forgetting the book with the moon. It took a while, but the path toward was not anything she could recall.

Tara recalled these discoveries. She thought to alert the two women of her presence and let them know of these and other wonders. For they were wonders, weren't they? They were sights people searched for, quested toward.

She was resolved to at least hint at it all to them. Secrets of the stars and the moons and the books they all lived in were not worth keeping. As she got closer, on the edge of the page, she saw their kiss. The way it blazed and gave light.

Maybe, Tara thought, maybe I should just move on. They wouldn't notice her walking by, would they?

So Many Midnights by Alix di Marquand

Yuri waited a few weeks before he went to the weekly gathering to talk to someone about it. He wandered the books. He didn't have a set address. There were always open books to head to. He just liked the way the words hung above him and the light through spaces showing a path to trod.

He got to the weekly gathering early, figuring he would ask his question, feel relatively satisfied and then leave. He spied Mojar talking to a group of new punk squatters. He stood near her and waited. In a few minutes she noticed him and excused herself.

"Can I speak to Terence, I found something in one of the books" Yuri said.

"Terence is, he's not here. The dude can be busy, you know. But I can hear it out and if it's important I'll get him in on it, fair?"

"Seems so. I was going around the books and I found something in a page break. Kind of weird. Thought you guys should know about it."

"Bones? Moons? Apple trees? There is always something being found out in the books."

"Motorcycles," Yuri said. "Bunch of motorcycles. 20 or thirty. Not kickstanded. On their sides. Weird insignias on them. Not Indians but Injins. Not Harley's but they read Hartley and Donaldson bikes. Weird, right?"

Mojar looked around quickly. "Show me."

After a pause, Yuri turned and walked out of the big anthology. Mojar followed. They walked through a copse of romance novels. Through a stream of space opera. They avoided the tough crags of the hardboiled books, taking the long way through the self-help paperbacks where the light was a warm greenish yellow. They took a break, drinking canteened water in some yellowing Shakespeare plays. "When I find myself here," Yuri said, mostly to himself, "I always figure that I'd speak better. More poetry in my words. Don't never work, but when I come across these volumes, I'm always a little bit hopeful. Aw hell, people can understand me, why do I want to sound pretty past that?"

The next leg was nothing but gothic romances. Hayden thought he saw the shade of a scared young nurse, but this stretch had phantoms, like most terrains of books do. Just that these had cleaner clothes.

They entered the right book. Mojar nodded to herself. "This is the one."

"Pardon? What you say?"

"I was here before. Long time. When it was me and Terence and a handful of others. I was here. I think it was here. Forgot what book it was, couldn't find it again. Which was alright by me. It's alright to lose things from time to time. Just toss it out the window while driving on the highway."

"What," Yuri asked. He had no idea what she meant. All he wanted was to tell Terrence about the bikes. He didn't plan on trekking through the books with Mojar. She was scary, and more silent than a blank page.

"I saw a bunch of motorcycles once out here. But only once."

Yuri stopped walking as realization hit him. "You don't think I'll be able to lead you to it. You think I'm not going to get you to this mirage again."

"Yeah. That's exactly what I think. But I haven't walked the far volumes in a long time. Nice to be out in the country."

They walked like old friends who never looked each other up anymore. Then they turned the page. They were there. Yuri was about to say something like, here it is or we're here or we made it, but he looked at Mojar and realized that there was no need. Why use words when a punk's got eyes?

Hayden didn't say anything but Mojar replied all the same. "Yeah. This is the place. Mostly."

There was no time to wonder why Mojar threw in that "mostly" in the end. The pile of motorcycles spoke up and bounced up and down on the balls of its feet.

There were thirty or forty bikes. There was a layer of dust. The books don't have dust, but the picture would be off if there wasn't a layer of dirt, so it was correct to have it. None of the motorcycles were upright. They were all knocked down. It was a definite realization, they were not put down onto the ground gently. These suckers were knocked down after they were abandoned. They used to be fine bikes, no one would have left them if they weren't fleeing for their lives.

The handlebars tangled into each other, as if holding hands while standing on a high ledge. The tires displayed the slash marks of a large blade. A screwdriver or a large nail punctured all of the gas tanks. The air didn't reek of gas, so all of this happened long ago.

"This is what it looked like when I was here. But you're right, Injun bikes. Not Indians. When i was here the insignias said Indians and Harley Davidson. Things deteriorate. That's what things do. They break down. But they don't change their names. They just rust it to forgetting."

"I don't know. Maybe it's books. Things wear out in a literary way. They break down, sure. They slowly change their words until they are brand new, in a broken down rusted way."

"Yuri, that's ridiculous."

"You're looking at a Hartley Donaldson chopper and calling this ridiculous? Why can't they just shed their own name like snake skin and get another design underneath." Mojar didn't respond, which made Yuri think that perhaps his guff actually made sense. Hell, there was a first for everything. He ran his finger on the burnished chrome. "Hey, why are there motorcycles here?"

Mojar circled the mass of entwined motorcycles a few times as if she was doing some rite of invocation. Silently. Slowly. She stopped. Looked at the bikes. "These books were old before Terrence stumbled upon them. No one looks to live in books. That kind of living is always an accident. He figured soon enough what he had. He got me and a few others. We explored. We brought other punks. Punks understand how to live between lines. Had to be punks. But that doesn't mean that Punks are the only kind of folk that thought of living here."

Yuri realized she was expecting him to make some connections, but he was tired from the trek and who could be expected to make mental leaps like this? And then, he got it. "The people who lived here before us. They were bikers."

"Yeah, I think so. But we never saw any of them, hiding out in a copyright page, or in an index. And we looked. Had to. If we were going to move in, and open it up to others, we had to be sure that our people wouldn't be jumped by a crazed biker. But they were gone. The only thing we knew of them, was this. This pile."

"So you're not sure that there were bikers at all. Maybe the bikes just grew from the page, like metal topiary. Maybe we are the only people who found this place."

Mojar turned and went back the way they arrived. She didn't make any move to invite him to follow her.

He stayed for a while. He tried to separate the bikes from one another. But it was like those metal puzzles he used to see at boardwalk gift shops. They say there is a solution, but after a few minutes of twisting and failing, Harden always knew that the solution was just not available for someone like him.

He knew he should move on, go about his travels. But he got himself turned around and ended up back at the bikes. Yuri felt different. Like things were changing. His name didn't feel like his own. Things were different in that familiar manner.

Ghostly Hoofbeats by Norman A. Fox

"I Iive in a book written by a guy named Norman A. Fox. The least I can do is honor him by taking my name from him," A. said to anyone he came across. "I couldn't allow anyone to call me Norman. I just couldn't do it. A name that square and ridiculous is pretty punk if you think about it that way, but I just couldn't do it. There was no way I was going to be Norman. Though I am hoping someone does, show us all up. I was thinking about being called Fox, but look at me. Look at this homely package. No one should look at me and say Fox. Even with irony. So I had no choice, I had to be the letter A."

This was how he typically introduced himself as he went from book to book. When he got to Rust's book, the speech sounded a little rote by this time. Rust almost heard the hiss and crackle of an old record as A. spoke. "Hey man," Rust said, interrupting the set speech, "I know exactly what you are spinning. I mean no one called me Rust when I was a kid. Mom didn't shoot me to dinner by bringing out the name Rust. I picked it. I gave it to myself. Best present I ever got. It's always the right color, and the size is perfect every time I put it on. And I didn't have to wrap it. Course my name is not an honor of any dead writer, though maybe I will say that it is from now on. Makes it sound better, don't it?"

A. nodded and continued on with the pleasant conversation. This was always the hardest part of the visits he was conducting. The talking about himself. Listening to the other person. There were many ways to feign attention. They were looking and smiling. A nod, a grunt at the right part of the conversation. A. understood and had all these methods defined and diagrammed in his mind. But he could not do any of it. He stood and listened and felt impatience because he didn't care why he was called Rust. For that matter, he didn't even care about his own biography. It really didn't matter that he named himself after the middle initial of a forgotten author. As a matter of fact, that might not even be true. A. was not completely certain why he began calling himself that. It might have been because of the author, but he had a vague memory of calling himself that one lone letter long before he even began to live in books. Maybe that was his name. Who can trust what anyone remembers about things? Even if those things are personal. Even if those things make up his name. Can anyone really lay claim to such certainty?

Rust and him were still talking banal talk and A. did not hear any of it. He was just figuring out how to move to the important part. The real part. The reason he visited everyone in their books. This might have been the twenty first visit he had made. All of this kindness, these birds of a feather geniality. It was hard. But if he didn't do it, he would never find out what he needed to know.

A. perceived a lull in the conversation. A pause that indicated that all of this useless talking could end. That maybe some useful words were allowed in for a brief visit. "Well," A. said. He found himself standing in another long pause. Rust was staring at him. "Well, I have a reason for coming by. For bothering you. I hope I ain't bothering you."

"You're not bothering me. You would know it if you were bothering me. But you're not."

"Good. Yeah. That's good. I don't want to be bothering people. I don't like people getting into me. So why should I get into them? It ain't right. That's what the other life is like. That's why we live here in books. So we don't have to be bothering people. That's why I live in books at any rate. I've been going and talking to people, the past couple of days. I think I bothered a couple of them. I didn't mean to. But people don't like to be disturbed. They live here after all."

"What can I do for you A? What are you looking into?"

"Okay," A. blew out air hard. "I was living in a book that was good. Kept me warm. Kept me fed. I read some of it, but it wasn't for me. I don't know if any of the books are for me when it comes to telling me something I need to know. But in the book was a wedged piece of paper. It was loose-leaf paper ripped up roughly and folded and jammed in between pages 76 and 77."

"Bookmark," Rust said.

"Yeah, that's what I thought. I walked by it for weeks and weeks, never giving it a thought. It was just a part of the landscape that you don't even notice after a while. Then one day, because I had a lot on my mind and a lot of things I wanted to do, I stopped and read it."

After a silence, Rust asked, "Did it say anything I needed to know?"

"I don't know that but I read it again and again. It was a to do list. But not to get milk or eggs or to fix the washing machine or to get more ammunition for the gun. This was a to do list on how to be a better person. Smart stuff. Good stuff. A list of ways to live that made sense to me."

A stopped talking again and Rust quickly jumped in to fill the pause. "What were these to dos? These self-improvement hints?

"I don't remember. That's the weird part. I read this list over and over. I couldn't get myself to stop pulling it out and reading. It became a compulsion. The constant rereading. I don't think I ever tried to follow these suggestions, but damned if I didn't want to read them as much as possible. One of the reasons I kept on reading it, kept on going back to it, was because it never came up when I tried to remember. The only way I had it was when I read it. Then it faded."

"Faded?"

"It was like the ink it was written began to pale. Not fade. It was more like someone being drained of blood. Getting wan. Then the draining became too intense and the words were no longer on the paper. They were somewhere else. They are not gone, because I don't think good ideas can just be gone, be missing. I think they moved somewhere else. So that's what I've been doing, going to people around here and asking if all of a sudden a good line of advice has shown up in their book that was not there before."

Rust smiled, "And you can't tell me what it said?"

"No. No I can't, but I figure that if anyone saw it, read it, they would know. There would be something they needed and be able to point the way for me."

Rust gave A. the look of someone thinking about a problem, though nothing of the sort was occurring. He was just trying to figure out how long it would take him to get this guy out of his book. And, unbidden, Rust remembered this woman he met a few weeks back. She was trying out this life and living in a translation of an Italian crime novel. She and Rust liked the look of each other and wound up naked and having sex. It was decent but he knew there was no distance to this race. He laid with her, on top of a soft paragraph of introspection. She had a lot of tattoos. More than any other woman he had been with. Her arms swarmed with lines of writing. Important texts that kept her sane, she said. He asked her about each line, each passage, and she told a long story about the people and the things that happened that made her put the line on her. Then he got to a line, a piece of advice, that was inked in what seemed to be blocky handwriting. The line was powerful, it made sense to Rust. He read it to her and she asked what that was. He read it to her again and said it was right there on her shoulder. She said that she didn't put it there. But it was good advice. Something to try to do. And she asked him to read it to her several times before she eventually fell asleep.

Rust thought about reading the line to the woman, but never the line itself. He couldn't recall, other than the realizing it was a good thing. Rust remembered all of this and felt something itchy and unwanted on his back, like a battalion of tiny ants clamping down on his shoulder blade. He wanted to tell A. this, ask him if this is what he was looking for. Rust said, "No, man. Sounds crazy. Never heard of anything like it. Never came across it. But, hey, thanks for thinking of me enough to ask." Which was a fine way to usher A. out of his book.

A. continued to the next book. And the next. And Rust just tried to forget the whole conversation but found it hard to.

Poisons Unknown by Frank Kane

Tomas was new to the books. He tried out a few books. Some by himself and some with others. None of this was bad, he just wasn't ready to say that this, this was his place. He tagged the back cover of every book he stayed in. It was his tag, the tag he always used. It was a Jackyl. That's what he said, Jackyl. "It comes from when I was a young and I used to run with corner boys and kids wearing matching bandanas and swinging regulation baseball bats at anything but a ball. I got the name Hyena from the way I laughed. I liked it. When I tagged a Hyena, no one knew what the hell I was doing. One guy said it was a Jackyl. Now I never took that as my name, cause I didn't want anyone coming up, slapping me on the back and saying Hi Jack. Wasn't going to risk that. I kept Hyena for as long as I with those stupid kids, never really liked it. But I kept my tag. My Jackyl. I want people to know I'm here."

Mikey, who was talking to him, said, "I hear you. You got something you like to draw that you feel is you, you keep on doing it. I'm that way. For a bit, I was drawing nurses. That was my thing. I probably can explain why I was drawing nurses all the time, but you don't want to hear all that. You just have to know that every artist has a thing, a theme. What is it? A motif. Mine was nurses. I did a lot with them and it led me to a few things that led me to the drawings I'm doing now: trees and bushes come out of concrete, or trying to. But that's not the point. The point is I wouldn't know that was a Jackyl or a Hyena or any African dog if you didn't tell me."

"No. No, that ain't right. That is my dog. That is my Jackyl."

"It's a mess is what it is," Mikey said. "I ain't saying there is anything wrong with big messes in art. I love it. I don't do it in my work, but I love when people can control what they are doing with the anarchy of it all. Anarchy is important to what we do here, I think. But man, you got a shaky on finished triangle for the head and squiggly lines on the top."

"That's the hair."

"And those jutting lines, are his ears? I don't get it. I don't want to be disrespectful, but it's a jumble of lines and angles and it adds up to what you want I suppose, but it ain't no dog, no Jackyl."

Tomas thought of turning his back on this idiot and walking out on him in a fierce manner, but it was better to not turn shoulder and just stare down this idiot. "Well you know Mikey, it don't matter what you think. Do I come over to you and say your trees look dumb stuck in the middle of sidewalks? I don't, because that's your art. That's the way you want the world to see your product, your thing. So do me the same. Don't like my tag and leave me alone."

Mikey looked right back into Tomas. "Can't do that, buddy. Wish. I was trying to convince you to quit the tags on aesthetics. But you like what you do, so there you go. Now I got to say, you are defacing the books and you got to stop."

"Wait," Tomas said slowly. He was figuring things out. "Wait," he said again. He was almost sure of what to say, not completely, but he figured he was going to lose Mikey if he said wait again. "Are you, well, are you saying that you ain't talking for yourself, you're talking for someone else? Is that what I got here?"

Mikey looked down at his shoes. They were covered in paint, which is the way he always liked them. He waited. Then said, "You're making tags on the books. Some folk might say that you are defacing the books, but we are not the kind of people, any of us, who would be upset about defacing public space. Defacing public walls is righteous art, and we are all for it. But this ain't public space. These are books. We ain't paying to live here. We were given these books as a gift. The least we can do is not muck it up with shaky paint."

"My lines are not shaky. They are clean and correct."

"That's not the point Tomas. Really. I know when Terrence or Mojar or whoever else introduced you to how you can live here, they didn't say, don't be a punk. Don't be an artist. But look at it this way. The books themselves are art. Even this lousy forgotten yellowing mystery paperback is art. The writer, the editor, the publisher, the drug store clerk who sold it for thirty-five cents, the lonely guy who bought the book, none of those folks thought that this thing was art. But that's the thing about art, no one needs to know that it's art, it's like the hand of God. Faith. Don't believe that these books are like a museum, but they are. They are museum building and the painting hanging on the walls."

"Now come on. You are definitely an artist, cause as a talker, you are making no sense at all. The books are museum pieces? That's crap. I went to that weird book where the chick painted over all the words. There was the book with the guy who pushed all the words into a big block and god knows what happened to him. And let's not even mention that we eat the punctuation. We live off of defacing this pristine and sacred art. Come on now. You were told by the ones holding the leash that they don't like my tag. Well, Mikey, tags were never meant to be admired. Tags is art just like a half dead guy screaming I am here, I am here, I am here, is art."

Mikey started to say something and then just laughed. "Dude. You are the worst tagger in the world. Your shit is lousy. And you put it everywhere. You got me. You're cluttering up the neighborhood. It's wrong of me saying this, but I believe all the same. Just put the damn spray can down and nobody will get hurt." Mikey must have thought something he said was funny, or at least he thought something was funny. He fell down to the ground laughing so hard. He wiped tears from his eyes and still laughed.

Tomas stood over the balled up figure of Mikey, racked with laughter. Tomas waited for the other to cease. To stop laughing. He waited. Mikey couldn't catch his breath. The laughter continued.

Tomas got bored. He went to the end of the book. He looked back one more time, Mikey was still giggling and gasping. Tomas took out his paint can and tagged the page. A Jackyl. The Jackyl.

"That shit looks good," Tomas said to himself. "Looks just fine. I'm here too."

Tomas let the can fall through his fingers. And then he split.

Hospital Librarian by Margaret Malcolm

Jo made a wedding dress from Chapter eleven. After reading the entire book several times, she decided that the best she could do, in terms of romance and volume, it had to be chapter eleven. It was the longest chapter, and she needed a lot of material for the dress. And in any of these old romance paperbacks, the longer the chapter, the more the romance. It was a simple equation.

She ripped up the pages into mostly uniform strips. She could have used Andy's knife and make the strips perfectly measured, but she wasn't looking for perfection in the dress, she was looking for beauty. Ah hell, who was she kidding, she just didn't want to speak to Andy, so ripping was easier.

She weaved the strips of chapter eleven together and made sheets of them. At this point she did use Andy's knife. She didn't ask him, no way. She boosted it. Served him right for being such an Andy. Jo knew that didn't make much sense, but she wasn't one for words and anger. She was for making things. And this wedding dress needed a good sharp edge to cut and mold the woven sheets into the right pattern.

It had volume, not just in length of chapter, but volume in that the dress took up space, and moved and breathed. It was elegant and right, but it was frilly or precious. Backless, and having one sleeve. The hem was slightly asymmetrical, but not so much that it became the center of the piece. This was a wedding dress that didn't need to apologize for itself. This was a wedding dress that had a side pocket that could hide a knife, a knife just like Andy's for example. Mean and fierce and filled with somebody else's words of love.

The perfect wedding dress. Now all it needed was for someone to wear it. It wasn't going to be Jo. She wasn't into marriage. But she did like making wedding dresses.

This was a concern about the community living in the backs of books. There were some couples, but there was no one wanting to get married. No one felt that there was a need for it. Sure, marriage was a piece of the patriarchal cancerous world they were escaping from. The world they rejected. Or maybe that world rejected them.

She found Des, a beautiful girl who was in love with Phaedra, and said, "When you two get married I have a hell of a dress. It's gorgeous."

"Yeah," Des said without looking up, "I want to see it."

That's how these things worked in the books. People stated something they came across and then someone else begged on to witness. To see something. To check it out in a book. These things are the way discovery has always worked. Be it a foreign continent or a way to turn lead into gold or to see a dire wolf or to check out a wedding dress made from a chapter of a romance paperback. The Viking warriors would have gotten it, they would have been at home living in a book, if you forgave them for insisting all their novels be printed in a runic alphabet. Vikings were almost punk enough.

"Wow." This was all Des said when she looked at the dress. "Wow." She walked around it. Kicked up the hem, to watch it shiver down into silence "Wow."

Jo smiled so large she felt compelled to cover it with her hand. "So you're going to wear it when you guys get married?"

"No."

"Uhm, okay. Phaedra. She'll wear it."

"Fraid not."

"What. You love it and neither of you will wear the wedding dress?"

"We're not a traditional wedding couple. We will probably just give each other rings and vows. Vows are nice. And rings are cool. Those two things. That's what we'll do. But wedding dress. I don't think so. It's pretty to look at it. And the amount of work. Jo, it's incredible art."

"I didn't make it to be looked at. I made it to be worn. And then it will be looked at. But a wedding dress is only beautiful when someone is wearing it at a wedding. It's location specific in its beauty."

"No, it's beautiful just the way it is. I could watch it for a while. I might visit it. But no. I ain't wanting to have me or Phae wear it. And don't bother asking her, I don't want you to be disappointed twice."

He did visit the dress every now and again. Well, she was visiting Jo, who was nice company. Jo didn't give up. She searched out couples living the book life and corralled them to check it out.

The conclusion she came to was, "Punks don't marry. And when they do, they don't wear awesome wedding dresses. Let me tell you. They are missing something terrific."

She took Missy by the hand to see the dress after it was revealed that Missy moved in with Dylan, that zine writer. Missy allowed herself to be dragged to the dress, but she didn't provide the expected oohs and ahhs all the others said. None of the others wanted the dress, but they still gave oohs and ahhs. But Missy was silent, she just nodded and said, "Yeah, chapter eleven, right?"

"Wait, what? Yeah. Wait. It was chapter eleven I used. How did you know that? The chapter heading isn't visible."

"Because it's always chapter eleven, all of them," Missy said with a shrug. "For all the chapter eleven dresses, this is a nice one, but it's still just a chapter eleven dress."

There was a time of quiet staring. Missy looked at her shoes, unsure of why things suddenly felt uneasy. Jo stared at her dress. Her beautiful, unique, amazing dress. "Are you telling me that there are dresses like this one, all made from chapter eleven of the books?"

"Uh, yeah. They just started popping up a couple weeks ago. No one's taking credit for it. Or blame for it. Terrence and Mojar are pissed. They don't like all these chapters up and turned into wedding dresses."

"Wedding dresses are beautiful."

"But nobody's taking it as their own and wearing them. They don't want whole chapters being destroyed."

"I know I made this one. I made this dress. But who's taking up my idea? Who's making more dresses no one wants," Jo said with a bit of a whine in her voice.

"I don't know. I thought there was a weird movement. That someone was just screwing with the community, knowing that Terrence was annoyed. But here it is, someone taking credit. Did you make any other dresses?"

Jo put her hands up and shook them, saying no-no-no-stop. "I made one, hoping someone would get married in it. Why make a wedding dress without a wedding? I could just make something else."

"Why didn't you?" Missy asked.

There was no answer to this, Jo realized. How could she answer something that was so obvious. Some chapters just demand to be made into certain things, and that chapter eleven required a wedding dress. That's all. There was still one problem. "Why is someone making wedding dresses like mine?"

"Maybe no one did," Missy suggested. "Maybe the chapter elevens in the other books saw what happened to your chapter eleven. They liked it and they changed into wedding dresses. Maybe they were all tired of being unread pages of forgotten books. Maybe they thought it would be a fun alternative to be a stylish wedding dress that will never be worn."

Jo spent the next month visiting the other wedding dresses. She asked around and folks directed her. She saw eight wedding dresses. They all seemed off. They had all the requisite parts. They had backs and corsets and skirts. Nothing was missing. Perhaps it was the dimensions. Maybe it was the ratio. But they felt like they were made by someone who had never seen a wedding dress before. By someone who never understood what a wedding dress was for. "Someone like me." She said to herself, though decided not to believe what she said.

When she returned to her book she went right to her dress. Her dress. She watched it hang there at the edge of the page for a while. Jo stripped out of her clothes. She slid into the dress. The dress fit, but it was uncomfortable. Moving around in it gave her a sense of bulk and several paper cuts.

Still wearing the dress, she went to the other chapter eleven wedding dresses. She went to each one and tore them all into small pieces. They each made tidy piles in the backs of the books they came from. Some indistinct wind picked up and the pieces flew into the air, traveling to all the books, even the uninhabited ones. The ones waiting for a mate.

About the Book

Finding a place to live is tough. There isn't a lot of places available, and when they are, they are crazy expensive. A group of punks and drop-outs have discovered the decent enough place to live: in the back of old paperbacks.

It is simple living, but there is no rent. And because people ignore old books, they are pretty much left alone. They eat punctuation and hunt animals that are also loose in the old books.

These stories are of those who live in these forgotten books. Some are there to hide-out or to work on their art. They are they to write zines and be off the grid. Things change in books though. Things can get weird. Reality can alter when you live in old books. You can turn into something else living in books.

About the Writer

David is the author of something like forty short ebooks. There is books on bar going,, "Gin and Tonics Across Worcester," and novels, "More Sopping Products," as well as strange ones that does not fit any category, "Orphan Stone Signs." He is the editor of the zine, The Long Weekend Review.

macphersondavid607@gmail.com
100pagedash.wordpress.com
On facebook David's group is Dave Macpherson is a Writing Stuff.
Instagram DavidScottMacpherson

20812